ROMANCE EDITION

NATASHA ROSE

This is a work of fiction. Unless otherwise indicated, all the names, characters, businesses, places, events and incidents in this book are either the product of the author's imagination or used in a fictitious manner. Any resemblance to an actual person's living, dead, or events is purely coincidental.

ISBN: 978-1-7636309-1-8

Dedication

I want to thank those who have supported me.

Table of Contents

Prologue

Two men stood face to face in a dimly lit alley, the tension palpable in the air as they exchanged a brief nod of recognition. One, a scruffy-looking dealer with a hardened expression, held a bag of drugs in his hand, while the other, a nervous buyer peeking over his shoulder, clutched a wad of cash.

As the transaction began, the dealer showed the buyer the bag of drugs, a glint of greed in his eyes as he eagerly gazed at the money. But then, the sound of sirens pierced the air, causing both men to freeze in fear.

Panic set in as the dealer realized they had been set up, and the authorities closed in on their illegal exchange. With a curse, the dealer made a move to flee, but the buyer, desperate to save himself, lunged forward and grabbed at the bag of drugs, refusing to let go.

A struggle ensued as the two men wrestled for control of the bag, the drugs spilling out onto the ground in a chaotic mess. The dealer's eyes widened in anger as he fought to regain possession, while the buyer, driven by fear and adrenaline, refused to back down and wanted to take it further.

During the chaos, a gunshot rang out, causing both men to freeze in shock. The dealer staggered back, clutching his side in pain, blood oozing through his fingers. The buyer, realizing the gravity of the situation, shoved the gun in his side pocket, dropped the bag of drugs and fled into the darkness, leaving the wounded dealer behind.

As the sirens grew closer, the dealer sank to his knees, the pain of his gunshot wound overwhelming him. He knew he had made a fatal mistake, one that had cost him dearly. The sound of approaching footsteps filled the alley, and with a heavy heart, the dealer closed his eyes, knowing that his once profitable drug deal had gone wrong, leading to a tragic and violent end. Moving quickly, he didn't want to go out for nothing, "I know who did this, and they're going to pay," he spat out of his gritted teeth to his other dealer on the mobile phone.

Chapter 1

Midnight. It always felt like it was midnight at the strip club. The thumping music bounced off the neon-soaked walls, drinks clinked and slammed on the tables. Darkness obeyed with stranger's desires and kept their faces hidden. Also, in their favour- the tables where lap dances were performed were light enough for the customers to see what they were paying for.

Midnight. It always felt like it was midnight.

Club *XXXtacsy*—stylized with a massive neon pink 'X' flickering and drawing men in—was so busy on a Friday night. The girls were worth it. They were beautiful and busty, bright-eyed, experienced, and very sexy. Delilah was one of them.

They called her Caramel because of her beautifully sun-tanned smooth skin. She had long dark brown hair, piercing blue siren eyes, seductively full lips and her breasts were round and natural—unlike most of the other girls with boob jobs and oversized BBLs—and her toned body curved perfectly.

She sat behind the vanity mirror in the dressing room, the lights beaming over her skin lighting up the dots of shimmer on her cheeks and cleavage. The dressing room was buzzing; a waft of sweet sultry pop star perfumes filled the air as the girls walked around ass-wiggling with their tiny lace panties on. Various girls were coming in with their huge duffel bags of disguise, dressed casually in baggy clothes, some in different stages of undress. Powder was clapped in between palms and rubbed onto thighs for gripping the pole.

"Hey Caramel" a blonde lady called out, waving at Caramel. Her name was Teagan. One of the cutest girls at the strip club, Caramel always thought. Plus, she was one of her only friends.

"Hey girl, kill it out there!" Caramel responded with a soft laugh.

"You know I will," Teagan said fluffing and teasing her long highlighted blonde hair up and down, posing at the front of the dressing room door with her ample ass peeking out of her short pink tartan pleated skirt.

Smiling, Caramel turned around and stared at her reflection again. She was topless, her nipples covered with a pair of shiny nipple star pasties.

Music boomed inside the club, trickling into the dressing room. The girls talked amongst themselves, giggling as they put on sparkling makeup, thrusting their breasts up in their bras and puckering their lips. Caramel loved to be on her own, away from the gossip and all that. Everyone liked her, sure— everyone was supposed to get along with everyone at the club; that was a rule—but she knew the girls sometimes talked about her, hating how much money she made on her shows. She didn't care. It was business, but being alone was always better.

She took a deep breath as she got ready for her show. Closing her eyes, pacing her breathing as she had done on so many occasions, she had a flash of when she first started. Years ago, just an innocent girl from a broken home, thrust into a murky world of sex and lust, forced to fend for herself. She shook away the thoughts, banishing them to the back of her mind.

Not tonight, Caramel, not tonight, she thought to herself. That time was long gone now; she felt in charge of her own story.

Her phone vibrated, and the screen came on. Her eyes moved over to it, and she reached for the phone. A quick scan of the message and her heartbeat faster.

She thought about the meeting she had a few days ago and the prospects of making more money. Why wouldn't she take the deal if she could leave the strip club and be on her own, making five times as much?

But the risks, she heard a tiny voice whisper in her mind. *Consider the risks.*

She sighed softly and closed her eyes again. She remembered where she had come from, the abuse, beatings, and poverty, and somehow it strengthened her. *What was a little risk?*

Opening her eyes again, a new resolve in her mind, Caramel typed a response to the text she had just read.

Sounds good. I'm in.

Caramel got on the platform just as her show was about to start. The place was rupturing with excited wolf whistles and shouts as she strutted in, her hips swaying seductively. She had done this so many times now it was easy to know what the men loved and how to get more money from them.

At this point, it was effortless.

She wore just a tiny string purple bikini. One of those metallic ones. Hair was set long and straight. The thick diamante choker around her neck was like a stripper's version of a royal crown, to let everybody know that she was the queen of the club, but they already knew that; they were waiting for her. The dimly lit room was then filled with hushed anticipation as the spotlight illuminated the tall, sleek pole that stood at the centre of the stage. The music began to swell, a sultry beat that set the tone for the performance that was about to unfold.

Lights flashed around her, red and blue and green flickering, and spinning, forming shapes and patterns before fusing into a concentrated spotlight resting on Caramel behind the stage curtains.

The men saw her silhouette at first, but then everything became bright, and she emerged with finesse. Her bikini glowed, showing the outline of herself as she was squeezed tightly by the fabric. They stared as Caramel did her thing— grabbing the pole and slowly swinging around, bending over to reveal her perky ass cheeks up against the shimmering material, rising again, grinding her body very slowly against the pole.

Looking back at the crowd with a confident smile, she approached the pole and wrapped her toned limbs around it, her body twisting and turning as she began to move in a mesmerizing dance. She executed flawless spins and twirls.

She climbed the pole with ease, her body soaring high into the air as she executed gravity-defying tricks and flips that left her dedicated audience in awe.

As the music reached its peak, she exited the pole perfectly to begin the floorwork of her show.

She smirked and glanced over her shoulders, still bent over, she lowered herself into the floor, she used her hand to pull up the strings of her bikini G-string onto her heels, lining it up to reveal her juicy ass as she thumped her hips on the floor. *They always like that,* she thought to herself with delight; turning around and grabbing the pole, she then lifted herself and began thrusting herself up and down the long steel in big, steep motions, staring at the crowd. She strutted near the front of the stage and heard the cheers from the crowd as she intensely scanned them with her sultry stare. The spotlight found her standing confidently on the stage. She stepped forward, her hips swaying in perfect time with the music, her eyes scanning the audience with a playful, knowing glint.

With a slow, deliberate motion, Caramel ran her hands up her sides, pausing at her waist to tease the onlookers, with their encouragement she kept going. Her fingers traced the line of her bikini top, accentuating the curves it barely contained. She danced closer to the edge of the stage, daring to get closer to her audience, who had dollar bills already clutched in their hands, ready for her.

Caramel turned, presenting her back to the audience, her hips rolling in a sensual rhythm. She looked over her shoulder, a sultry smile playing on her lips as she reached behind her neck. Her fingers toyed with the strings of her bikini top, drawing out the moment, and heightening the anticipation. The crowd leaned in; eyes fixed on her every move.

With a decisive flick, she untied the knot at her neck, holding the fabric in place with a single hand. She turned to face the crowd again, her free hand trailing down her body, amplifying the tease. Slowly, she released her grip, letting the top fall away. Silent gasps and loud cheers erupted as she revealed her perfect breasts.

Caramel's eyes met those of the front row, her smile deepening as she continued her dance, now freed from the confines of her top. Her movements became bolder and more expressive as she revelled in the energy and admiration radiating from the audience.

As the music built to its climax, Caramel moved to the center of the stage, dropping to her knees in a final, dramatic pose. As her hands moved up, she squeezed her smooth breasts, her chest rose and fell with her breath, her nipple pasties glimmering under the stage lights. Caramel could feel the crowd's energy; their excitement was like a thunderous wave that washed over her. They showed their appreciation for her as dollar bills flew in front of her.

Caramel stood with a final, triumphant smile and gathered her discarded top. She blew a kiss to the audience and gave a wink as a promise of more to come before exiting the stage, leaving behind an electrified room. Thankfully, the loyal security guards always picked up for her and gave her stack afterwards.

She never wanted to be seen scrapping the money off the floor at the mercy of the crowd; they needed her. She never wanted to show that she needed them.

The other girls in the dressing room spoke in hushed tones as soon as Caramel returned. It always sucked for the ones who had to go up after her, but again she didn't care. She caught a few sour looks as she counted a stack of bills. Her phone buzzed again. She was about to check it when the manager stepped in. He was a short man in a bright red suit, his fingers adorned with fake gold rings—even though he liked telling everyone that it was gold.

"Hey, Caramel, I need ya," he said, thrusting his chin at her.

She sighed and frowned, turning around. Her bare breasts jiggled slightly from the motion.

"I'm getting ready to leave, Zack, I wasn't even supposed to be working tonight," she said.

Zack raised a brow disapprovingly. "Well, you're just gonna have to wait a few more minutes. Some big shots liked your performance; they wanna see more of you."

"I'm not a hooker, Zack. I'm a stripper."

Zack grinned. This was an argument he'd heard so many times. The chicks always wanted to keep their dignity—or whatever was left of it—but he knew the right price would always sway them.

"Big shots, I said. Just hear 'em out. You don't have to agree to anything," he responded and turned around, disappearing as quickly as he left.

"I sure as anything would jump at any offer I get right now," one of the girls said without looking at Caramel.

Groaning softly, Caramel took off her nipple pasties, grabbed a purple mesh see-through top and stood up. Her round breasts thrust forward, hugged by the top, and her areolas were visible, the pointy nipples enough to attract any man's attention. Caramel liked to tease them because she knew, in the end, they would never have her.

She let her dark hair fall to her shoulders. A quick glance at the mirror and she was satisfied. Caramel left the dressing room.

Walking across the main area in her clear platform stiletto heels, one of the girls was performing on stage, shaking her behind while a group of bored-looking guys drank beers and conversed.

The night was wearing on, creeping into the early morning hours; things usually slowed down at this point.

Glancing up, Caramel spotted Zack, the manager. He gestured at the VIP corner, where the big shots were. She nodded and went in that direction. Years ago, she would have been nervous—wealthy men had a way of putting someone down, making them their bitches and all that—but she knew how much power her beauty gave her now; she could stay in control.

A couple of guys whistled as Caramel walked toward the VIP corner. Two burly guys in plain clothes stood outside the section, the guys inside talking and laughing out loud. They looked like important money-types all right, Caramel realized even from a distance. *They should get hookers, not me..unless they're looking for something else...*

She was just about to take another step when the first gunshot went off.

The explosive sound rippled through the air, and screams followed. The girl on the platform started squealing. She tried to run, but her ankle twisted on her high heels, and she fell off the platform, thudding on the ground.

Rapid gunfire lit up the club, the air choking with screams and a sense of fear. Caramel hid behind a table, her heart thumping fast. Loud voices rent the air, the gunshots spitting out like strings of firecrackers lit up simultaneously. Caramel crawled slowly, her ears ringing from the gunfire. Everyone was flattened on the ground, tables and chairs were overturned. Bottles shattered and smashed all around as bullets flew through the air.

Caramel glanced up, her hair falling over the side of her face. The manager, Zack, was a few steps away from her. He was

still on his feet quivering—*although his short ass makes it look like he's already kneeling,*

Caramel thought in a slight moment of amusement. A man standing in front of Zack suddenly grunted and hit the ground.

"He's been shot!" Zack screamed and fell. "I've been shot."

Caramel quickly crawled over to Zack. He was whimpering and shaking, clutching his arm.

"I've been shot!" he kept repeating.

Caramel saw the blood, but after touching the spot, she quickly realized it wasn't Zack's. It must have sprayed from the bleeding guy groaning on the floor, crawling away.

"Shut up and calm down!" she whispered to her manager, still making her voice firm enough. A few minutes later, the sounds of police sirens flooded the club, and the shooters made for the door.

Zack's face was as red as his suit when Caramel helped him up.

"This is a damn mess," he kept grumbling. "Now the cops are here. I'm ruined."

"What happened?" she asked him. He grunted and walked away.

Caramel stood up and looked around. Zack was right. It was a mess; although she had an idea, he was talking about something else. There were people slowly getting up, drunk and shaken.

The cleaning staff would have their hands full with all the broken bottles everywhere.

Blue and red lights beamed in from outside, this time very different from the alluring lustful vibes of the regular colorful lights inside the club. The cops were always bad news.

Caramel buckled slightly on her feet, her knees aching. A slight sting on her right elbow made her check, and she saw a graze there. Cursing under her breath, she brushed off the shards of glass and tried to get away as the place became filled with cops.

She staggered as she went back to the dressing room. She grabbed a bottle of cool water and gulped it down.

"Shit!" she said, sucking in a deep breath when she saw how much her hand fidgeted. Her chest ached from how rapidly her heartbeat was, and the echoing sounds inside her head made it seem like the gunshots had resumed. She closed her eyes, and all she saw was chaos, with the screams getting louder in her mind.

A petite pillar box redhead lady named Butterfly poked her head into the dressing room.

"There you are. The cops are everywhere, and they're asking all sorts of questions," Butterfly said, her face pale and her eyes full of fright. "Zack said not to say anything."

Caramel bit her lip and nodded. "You, okay?"

The lady shook her head and sniffled. "Terrified. I was..."
"Hey, it's alright, it's over now," Caramel said softly, heading over to the door where the lady was. She hugged her colorful tattooed body and told her to go home as soon as possible.

Butterfly sighed and nodded. "Oh, I'm sorry, but Teagan is injured. I saw them taking her into an ambulance."

She hurried off. Shaken, Caramel sat herself down again.

The club soon got quiet—she was the last one around, the silence almost comforting; anything was a welcome change from the chaos of screams and gunshots. A knock on the door suddenly rattled her. For one, no one ever knocked. She gasped and looked up, a part of her mind expecting a stranger with a gun glaring menacingly at her. A stranger showed up all right, his blue eyes glowing when he entered the room and saw her.

"I uh, hi," he stuttered, his top button loose and his smile cute and shy. Caramel sat up and mustered a faint smile taken by the handsome stranger. "Hi." She replied.

Chapter 2

Detective Salt was frozen when he set his eyes on the lady in the dressing room. He wanted to be professional, but there was something about her that shook him. Was it her eyes or the way her glossy lips parted slightly when she saw him? His eyes strayed down to her chest, watching the swell of her breasts.

"You don't have to be frightened," he said, fumbling for his ID.

He smiled. "I'm a cop. I'm not gonna hurt you. I just want to talk."

The lady sighed and nodded, relaxing in her seat. Salt puffed his cheeks, ushered himself fully into the dressing room and exhaled. He felt like his younger self, the awkward teen who'd blush when he walked in on a naked woman many years ago.

"My name is Salt," he said. "Detective Salt."

She smirked, raising her mesmerizing eyes to him. "Caramel."

He thought she was teasing him at first. He'd gotten that so many times before, especially growing up.

"I'm being serious. At least that's what they call me here," she added, reaching into a silver purse. She took out a red pack of cigarettes and, holding it in her slightly shaky hand, she tried to light up.

"Damnit!" she cursed as the lighter sparked without coming on.

"Here, let me help," Salt said, taking her hand and sliding the lighter off her grasp. They both glanced up at the same time, eyes locking at that sudden touch. He smiled at her and, composing himself, helped her light up her smoke.

She closed her eyes and savored the taste, smiled, and leveled her gaze on him. "Thank you."

Her voice was soft and pleasant, just as beautiful as her face.

"You're welcome," he finally said.

She cleared her throat after taking a few puffs.

"Just so we're clear, I don't trust you; you're a cop, I'm a stripper. I think you see the divide."

He chuckled and offered a friendly smile, sticking one hand in his pocket—partly to control the swell of his member. Her breasts, and the way they jiggled and swayed as she talked, sent so many feelings rushing through his body. Her dark-colored areolas surrounding those pointed nipples made it even harder.

I can see why they call her caramel-wait! You have a job here, focus he cautioned himself.

She narrowed her eyes, smoke swirling over her face, watching the detective. He blushed and smiled that shy smile. It made her curious about the man; there was something innocent about that smile, she thought. He also observed an innocence in the depth of her hot gaze, almost as if she wasn't meant to be in this place.

"So, what do you wanna ask?" she asked, flicking the ash from her cigarette.

Salt fumbled slightly, almost dropping his note. Caramel smiled, and he cleared his throat again, putting on his serious face. He went over the routine questions with her, and she answered sincerely, sighing a couple of times when she recounted the shooting.

"I guess that will be all," Detective Salt said, rising to his feet. He paused in his stride and looked at Caramel. "It's pretty late, when are you going home?"

She shrugged and licked her lower lip, suddenly feeling nauseous from the cigarette taste.

"Teagan's in the hospital. She was my ride. I guess I'll Uber." Salt checked the silver watch on his wrist, frowned and shook his head. "It's pretty late; how about I give you a lift?"

Caramel smirked, her lips poised in a sexy smile. "A real gentleman. You don't have to." "I insist," he said.

Smiling softly, Caramel stood up and turned around. Salt held his breath. *Look at that ass*, the voice in his head whistled. He couldn't take his eyes off the juicy curves of her body—the way her G-string slipped between the crack, the cheeks of her ass swallowing up the thin fabric, made him feel more aroused than ever before. She bent over to pick up a towel, and he got a slight view of her privates from the back. It drove him wild.

"I just need to have a quick shower; hope you don't mind?" Caramel explained, glancing over her shoulder. Detective Salt straightened up; his cheeks flushed.

"No, of course not. Take your time."

She smiled and said quietly, to herself, "A real gentleman; it's a nice change."

Turning her back to him, she slipped off her top. The Detective got a side view of her breasts from the mirror. She then wrapped the towel around her waist and took off her G-string, raising one foot after the other as she stepped out of it.

She walked out of the dressing room and entered the shower.

"Damn, that was crazy," he muttered under his breath as soon as he heard the shower running. He paced around, breathing hard, running his hand through his slick hair and puffing out his cheeks. He was hard, alright, and he couldn't take the image of Caramel's sexy body out of his mind. *No wonder these guys come here and blow all their money,* he thought with awe.

He paused, the soft sound of the shower drawing his attention. As if controlled by an unseen force, his feet suddenly led him towards the shower. He swallowed hard, getting aroused and his heartbeat pounding. The shower had a glass door, and she'd left it open, probably afraid after the shooting. He caught a glimpse of her body under the water, her hair wet and her skin glistening as drops of water trickled down.

She turned to the side, her nipple pointed, her breasts heaving. Her hands moved along the side of her body and up to her breasts, kneading softly with slippery soapy suds as she showered.

Detective Salt clenched his fist and moved away; the best he could do was to stop himself from rushing in there, pinning the stripper against the wall and ramming his body against hers to give it to her.

She'll like that...she's a stripper, remember? The voice in his head whispered. He eagerly watched her, knowing that it was so wrong, but so hard to resist.

'*What the hell are you doing?*' he asked himself, suddenly feeling like his younger self years ago when he'd stumbled upon his sister's friend in the nude, the image permanently burned into his mind.

The shower stopped, and Caramel stepped out.

Detective Salt panicked and froze.

His eyes widened as he stood face to face with a completely naked Caramel, her body wet and shiny.

"Oh, I'm sorry," he apologized and spun around, his cheeks flushed again. Those few seconds were enough to keep the image of her breasts in his head. Caramel giggled. "You're cute."

It took her a few minutes to change into her clothes.

"You can turn around now," she said, and he did so, smiling as he ran his hand through his hair and tried to act 'normal'.

'Oh, damn,' he said in a suppressed voice, she wore a white t-shirt and blue tight-fitting jeans. Her hair was clipped at the back, leaving a few strands falling over her face.

"You look...different," he said, unable to take his eyes off her.

She smiled.

"You can also call me Delilah," she said softly. "That's my real name. But uh, well, whichever you like."

Detective Salt chuckled. "They're both beautiful," he said, and she looked up, parting her hair and tucking it behind her ear. She had a curious look on her face, watching to see if he was being sincere.

She shrugged and lit another cigarette. "Guys use the word beautiful all the time, especially when they want to get between your legs," she said, placing the thin cigarette delicately between her naturally plump lips. "To have sex you, that is." Salt shuddered at the raw use of that word 'sex'.

The way she emphasized it made him shiver with something deep, something puzzling. It sent a shockwave through his body, making him most erupt. He could listen to her say that word all day.

It was cold outside as the car zoomed down the road.

Detective Salt took his time to explain a few things to Delilah. "I have a feeling this drug operation runs deeper than we actually think," he said gravely. He turned and looked at her.

"Someone is working from the inside. People don't usually hit up busy places like that unless they want to send a serious message."

Delilah paused for a second and looked away. "You mean like one of the girls?" she asked.

"We'll see," Detective Salt responded.

He finally got to her apartment in a rough neighborhood. They passed a couple of guys smoking and banging loud music.

"Is it always like this?" he asked, watching the way their heads turned as the car moved by.

She shrugged. "It's quiet most times."

"I doubt it," he said, his cop instinct kicking in. He stopped the car, and Delilah got out.

"Are you going to be alright out here?"

"That's cute, but I'm safe. You don't have to act like I can't handle myself."

"I just, uhm…I have to make sure and…"

"Would you like to come in?" she asked, halting his words.

"Yes."

Damn, that was too fast, he scolded himself. But that smile, lustful and enchanting, it pulled him in. It brightened up her face and made her look like some kind of angel sent to tempt him.

She took his hand and led him in. He turned around and glanced hesitantly at his car.

"It'll be there when you get out," she assured him, her hand soft around his. "Hopefully."

The door clicked shut behind them, and he became very aware of being alone in the same space as this beautiful woman. He was still wondering what to say when she spoke.

"So… I saw what you did," Delilah said, turning to him, her eyes sparkling. Her smile was teasing and so sexy.

"Uh, what?"

"You were watching me in the shower... I saw you checking me out. Wish you would've let yourself in..."

"Oh, damn. I'm sorry. I have no idea what came over me and I...wait, what?"

"You heard me," she whispered, eyes twinkling.

She stepped closer and then placed her hands on his chest, getting closer to him. He swallowed hard, feeling the heat surging through his body.

"I don't know if we should—"

"Don't be that guy. Not now, okay," she said with a slightly serious tone.

His thumping heart made him anxious, but he took a deep breath and had it under control. She brought her lips right next to his ear as she whispered, "How about we have a shower here together? I know you want me..I want you too"

She did not have to ask twice. He pulled her close and crashed his lips into hers, tasting the sweet flavor of her gloss. She moaned and kissed him back, her body shaking with emotion as she melted in his arms.

Delilah took control and led him into her shower. After turning the knobs of hot and cold on, they feverishly undressed, the rustle of clothing hitting the tiles echoed softly. Steam filled the bathroom, the warm water cascading down from the shower-head, created a soothing symphony. They stepped in together, the heat enveloping them as they stood facing each other, water droplets glistening on their skin.

Salt reached out, his fingers tracing the curve of her shoulder, trailing down her arm. "You're incredible," he murmured, his voice thick with insatiable emotion.

Delilah smiled, her eyes locking with his, "Hmm so are you," she whispered back, looking him up and down her hand coming up to rest on his chest, feeling the steady beat of his heart.

They moved closer, the water running over their bodies, heightening every touch. His hands travelled down her sides, exploring every curve, while she did the same, her touch light and teasing. They shared a deep, lingering kiss, the warmth of their bodies melding with the heat of the shower.

Breaking the kiss, Salt guided her hand down, his eyes never leaving hers. Delilah understood, her fingers wrapping around his length, stroking gently. He mirrored her action, his hand moving in deep to explore her, their breaths quickening in unison.

They kept eye contact, the build up of climax between them intensifying with each passing moment. Every touch, every caress, was with desire, a silent conversation of their true feelings.

As the sensations built, their gasps and moans mingled with the sound of the water, creating an intimate atmosphere between the walls. They brought each other closer to the edge, the intensity of their shared passion binding them even tighter.

When they finally reached the peak together, they held each other close, the diminishing minutes of their pleasure pumping through their bodies.

In the warm haven of the shower, they stayed entwined, the water washing away everything but the new interest they shared with each other.

After walking inside her adjoining bedroom, Salt peeked outside the window "You were right; nothing happened to my car," he called out with a grin, towel wrapped around his waist,

"There were the odd car backfires in the neighbourhood now and then, but I take you didn't hear them angel."

Early morning had come upon them.

"Don't be too sweet," Delilah said, coming out of the shower into the bedroom, wondering why this man's words made her feel weird and...special. "I'm no angel." She huffed as she sat down on the bed.

"Maybe not," he said, sitting beside her and gently tucking her freshly washed hair behind her ear. "But you sure are beautiful."

They stared into each other's eyes for a few seconds, then he looked away. "I'm sorry. I don't mean to come on too strong.

You don't do this after a fling, saying sweet words and all."

Delilah bit her lip and frowned, lowering her head and tucking the towel tighter to her chest. "A fling...yeah, you're right."

"I guess I better be going," he said, reaching for his shirt, sounding hesitant and his movements slow.

"You don't have to go so soon? Do you?" Delilah said. She was curious about him, and the idea of kissing him again made her heart pound and her body twinge with arousal.

He agreed, moving closer to her, slowly releasing her towel from her body.

He gently pulled her toward the bed, their damp bodies reflecting the soft glow of the bedside lamp. They laid down together, facing each other, the cool sheets a contrast to their heated skin.

She reached up, her fingers caressing his cheek, tracing the line of his jaw. He breathed heavy, his eyes locked with hers, inviting her to another intimate moment.

Their lips met in a slow, tender kiss, the taste of water and wanting mingling between them. His hand travelled down her back, pulling her closer, feeling the press of her curves against him. She responded eagerly, deepening the kiss.

They explored each other with a renewed sense of vigor, their hands roaming freely, re-discovering every inch of each other's bodies.

Delilah kissed a path along his neck, savoring the taste of his skin, while his hands traced the curve of her waist, drawing her closer. Their bodies fit together perfectly, the heat between them igniting a fire that had nothing to do with the shower's warmth.

As they continued to kiss, time seemed to stand still. It was just them, lost in the sensation of their closeness, the world and its new problem's outside forgotten.

Eventually, they pulled back slightly, their foreheads resting together, breathing in sync. They stayed like that for a while, wrapped in each other's arms, savoring the afterglow of their shared passion they felt.

She closed her eyes and moved down to rest her head on his chest, breathing gently.

"You're so beautiful, Delilah," he said quietly, expecting no response. Her heart skipped a beat.

The morning moved by quickly, with it came a new wave of feelings—one of guilt and... something else, something deeper.

The way he called her beautiful made her shiver. *They're just words; you get told stuff like that all the time,* she tried to remind herself sternly.

"I really have to go now; work calls," Salt said as he got up to get dressed. Delilah lifted her head and was about to say something in protest when the door suddenly swung open, and two men burst in. Salt jumped to action and threw himself at one of the men, knocking him against the bedroom wall.

The struggle lasted a few seconds as Salt punched the masked man in the gut and slammed his head into the wall, knocking him out.

"Look out!" Delilah screamed as the second guy aimed a gun at Salt. She quickly grabbed a heavy vase and smashed it bluntly against the guy's head. A loud crack followed.

Panting, Salt looked up at her and smiled. "That's gonna be one heck of a headache. We need to get you out of here. It's not safe, quick grab what you need."

Later that night, Delilah's phone lit up. A text.

WHAT THE HELL WAS THAT ALL ABOUT? YOU GAVE US THE ADDRESS! WE HAD THE MAN! YOU

BETTER HAVE A GOOD REASON FOR PULLING THAT SHIT.

She sighed and looked out the window, staring at the shining lights of the motel parking lot. *"What have I done?"*

She always resonated with a fox, swift and cunning. Now, she felt more like an owl. Her eyes observed the world below and all its complications. *I did this, and now I have to get out. Can I even get out? Is it too late?* She thought.

Chapter 3

At the police station, Senior Detective John Michaels stared at the evidence board, his mind racing with the pieces of the puzzle he had been trying to solve for weeks. The case involved a string of drug deals and shootings in the city, all connected by a series of intricate clues that led nowhere.

Detective John couldn't shake the feeling that more players were involved than the usual suspects. There might be a drug syndicate in his town... but who?

Detective John's heart raced as he replayed recent conversations in his mind, searching for any hint of guilt or deception in the criminal's interviews. *He has to find out the truth.*

Detective Salt leaned against a desk, white-knuckled, a puzzled look on his face. They'd had briefings on the case too many times to count now, and it followed them back home. Just like John, Salt needed to find the truth.

"This whole thing bothers me," Detective Salt finally spoke, prying John away from his relentless thoughts. John looked at him. "Yeah?"

"It looks like any other typical drug operation, with the lowlifes and shady nightclub owner, but perhaps that is just what they want us to think."

John stroked his chin. A few days stubble lined his face. Salt had shaved the night before, having glanced at the mirror, his tired reflection startling him. *Perhaps John didn't have a mirror at home,* he thought.

"How about her?" John asked, pointing to Caramel's picture from the board. "She's linked to this somehow, and I bet in a bigger way than she's letting you think- they targeted her apartment, for God's sake."

"Caramel...I mean, Delilah could be innocent of all this. Just another stripper caught in the middle of drugs and crime and all that."

John narrowed his eyes, frowning as he shook his head slowly. He grabbed a cup of his now-cold coffee and sipped, his face tightening at the cool bitterness spreading inside his mouth. "You know you're supposed to be objective, right? Look at the facts unbiased, dig deep and most importantly, no emotional attachments."

Salt knew he was going to say that. "You're right," he said. "I'm just saying she could be a red herring." "Or she could not," John chimed in.

Salt nodded, a determined look on his face. "I'll have to talk to her." His heart thumped at the thought of going to meet Caramel. *What the hell?*

He moved away from the desk and headed for the door. "If she knows something, I'll get it out of her."

John smirked. "Using your 'ol schoolboy charm, huh? Watch it so that you don't end up getting charmed yourself."

"Don't worry about me. Follow up on the other leads. I have a good feeling we're on the brink of something big." He called out

"Me too," John mumbled.

The motel diner was almost empty. It was small, having just a couple of tables, but neat and almost homely. Lights beamed down from the ceiling, casting a soft glow on the surprisingly well-polished red leather chairs, the sky-blue colors popping out of the large windows. A few diners came in and went out; a beautiful woman sat alone at a corner table, eyes on her phone as she ignored the food before her.

Salt scanned the place and spotted her. *Smart girl,* he thought. The table was secluded but gave a cautious view of the front door. He approached her. She looked up and smiled at him as soon as he got to the table. It was a sexy smile, bold and inviting.

He sat. They went through the usual pleasantries, taking for a few minutes. She had placed her phone facedown, not once lifting it as they spoke. She focused on him with eagerness and intrigue, which almost made him shy, but he wanted to meet with her for a reason. He had to get to questioning.

'Tell me the truth."

Those were Salt's words after he handed Caramel a tall cup of hot black coffee. He frowned when she took out a cigarette and lit it up.

"Don't give me that look, okay?" she said softly, her eyes shifting away from him. "I'm not a saint; no one is."

"I'm not judging."

She sucked in deeply, inhaling smoke and letting it fill the inside of her cheeks, then she let the clouds puff through her nostrils and smiled a sad smile.

"That look on your face, I know it all too well. Don't try to be a savior. Not everyone needs a hero." She said snarky. Salt was perplexed by her words. But most importantly, he wanted to prove to her that she'd figured him all wrong. He wasn't about to judge her for her life decisions; heck, he wasn't perfect.

As he sat opposite to her and took her hand gently. "Are you mad at me?"

She still had a smile on her face, but it was stiff and unfriendly. "You *are* mad at me," he said.

She smoked for a few minutes, and he waited patiently, saying nothing as he observed her beauty. He wanted to take her away, keep her safe and far from this whole mess. But he had to know what she knew, and he was sure she knew something. "I'm tired," she said softly, finally speaking. She squashed the half-burnt cigarette between her fingers. "So tired, I mean, you sure kept me up the other night," she added and sighed deeply, sinking into the back of her seat, her breasts jiggled slightly from the motion.

Salt couldn't take his eyes off her chest for a moment. She wore a light blue cotton top, which was nearly transparent, showed she was wearing nothing underneath. Her nipples pressed visibly against the top; the curves of her breasts very much visible. Moving his eyes lower, past her belly button— and the silver ring pierced into it—Salt noticed that she wore just a tiny jean skirt. *Surely, she wasn't comfortable in that,* he thought. Her thighs were bare, and he could see the outline of her panties. A matching light blue color, tiny and showing off a cheeky camel toe.

Damnit! He muttered under his breath, feeling his member pulse through his pants. *This is gonna be harder than I thought.*

There was something more than the physical attraction, that kept him wanting her more and he knew it. Sure, he wanted to pounce on her right there and have her like she'd never had before, but he also had to do his job.

Caramel's voice broke his thoughts. She had a sly smile on her face.

"You can ask me questions all you want...but I know your mind is elsewhere" she said.

He gulped, startled. "What?"

She chuckled as she stretched out a French-manicured finger and pointed at his crotch.

Salt's cheeks flushed. He was stretching across his pants, and he had no idea. How embarrassing!

"I guess I can't help it that you're so beautiful."

The way he said *beautiful* made her shiver. She loved the word, the softness of it.

"We could leave if you want...go back to my room?" she said with a mischievous twinkle in her eyes.

Salt smiled. "There'll be time for that. For now, just answer my question. Okay? I am a cop, after all."

She rolled her eyes and giggled. "Boring."

He also laughed. They sipped coffee and talked about random stuff. After a while, as he changed positions of his seat so he could be closer to her, she leaned her head closer to his side and rested it on his shoulder.

"I'm scared," she said softly.

"Why?"

"I…I don't know."

Salt squeezed her hand. "I know this goes against everything as I'm not supposed to be here like this, but you can trust me. It's my job to put the bad guys away, so just tell me everything you know, and I'll make sure nothing happens to you," he said softly.

"Promise?" she asked, looking up.

"I promise." He sworn.

He kissed her forehead, and she blushed, feeling a rush, she'd never felt before.

She wrapped her arms around him and found his lips. He wanted to question her and get everything she knew, but the temptation was so hard to resist. He kissed her back, her lips warm and sweet, the faint hint of cigarettes lingering. "Let's get out of here. I can't do what I wanna do to you here," he said softly.

Chapter 4

B ack at the motel room, it was on. They kissed passionately at the door entrance, knocking into the walls caressing each other, Until Salt broke apart from her. It was difficult, but he had a job to do. "No, no! Stop!! I'm here to ask you questions. You keep avoiding it!" He sat down sternly on the bed, and she joined beside him. They sat on the edge of the bed, tension hanging in the air. His eyes were filled with concern and confusion, his questions pressing down on her.

"Why won't you tell me what's going on?" he asked, his voice a mix of frustration and worry.

She sighed, feeling the weight of his words. She hated to see the anger building up in his eyes. She had to take control of the situation..and quickly.

Moving closer, she placed a gentle hand on his chest, her fingers tracing soothing patterns. "Let's not do this tonight, we have so much more time for all that later" she whispered, her voice soft, trying to bridge the gap between them.

Salt looked at her, conflicted, his guard still up. Delilah leaned in, kissing him softly, trying to convey her affection and need for closeness. He responded, hesitantly, the tension between them easing just a fraction.

Without breaking the kiss, she began to move down, her lips trailing a path along his neck and then to his chest. He watched her, his breath catching, the questions in his eyes slowly replaced by a different kind of intensity.

She continued her descent, trying to draw him into the moment. As she reached his waist, she glanced up at him, her eyes full of intent. His breath hitched, and he swallowed hard, the emotional turmoil giving way to a growing need.

With an exquisite slowness, she began to please him, her movements focused and deliberate, wanting to bring him intense pleasure and to distract him from the case. He let out a low groan, his hand tangling in her hair, his questions fading into the background.

She focused on him entirely, hoping to replace his doubts with pleasure.

As he reached his climax, the tension finally left his body, as she swallowed every drop of worry. He pulled her back up to him, their foreheads resting together. He looked into her eyes, the heated yearning between them so visible.

"We'll talk later," she promised, her voice a whisper. "But for now, let's just be here, together. Ok?."

"Ok yeah you're right ok" he said with a panting sigh

This ought to shut him up for a bit, snapped Caramel in her mind as she held him close.

Chapter 5

Detective Salt reported back nothing to his superiors. They had been investigating shady strip club owner Zack Massoni for several months, watching his comings and goings as they built up a solid case against him. They just needed to get to the main villain, the guy pulling the strings. Zack wasn't the main guy. But so far, it was proving difficult. But Delilah now seemed to be the missing piece in the puzzle.

"It'd make sense that they'd want to take her out, as she is close to the main source," Senior Detective John, said. This startled Salt, even though it was something he already knew. He had gone through her phone without finding anything definitive, but there had been a call from a private number.

That was suspicious. There had also been a text from Zack—**Don't say nothing**. He would need to look into it again if there had been any changes but ultimately, she knew something, and they were trying to shut her up. Salt suddenly felt desperate to get back to her. He was certain he could get her to talk, but he first had to make her feel safe. And damn it, he was beginning to grow attached to her, long for her in ways he hadn't felt in many years.

He spent the day going over files and everything they had on the case with his partner, then checked his watch and said he had to go.

Senior Detective John eyed him suspiciously. "Let me guess, back to her?" he called out.

"What?" Salt asked, feigning ignorance as he put on his jacket. "The girl...the stripper. I know about you two. I know you drove her home that night of the shoot-out. I saw her get into your car." John called out.

Salt stood still and silently.

"I'm a good cop like you, pal. And that's the thing: you're a good cop; don't let anything—or anyone—distract you. This could be the big one." John chuckled

"I know..."

"Hey, if the big one comes at the expense of the girl, then you know what choice you gotta make. She is just a stripper." *That girl...just a stripper.* Salt angrily clenched his jaw at those words, but then he took a deep breath and let it slide. It would make no sense to try to get John or anyone to understand. But then again, what if he was right? Salt sighed and nodded, leaving the office. He felt a leap in his chest when he thought about driving all the way to see her. It would take an hour, but it'd be worth it.

He got into his dark blue Tesla, still getting used to the machine, and drove off. He was so preoccupied with the anticipation and the weight of everything else—he knew now that she had something to do with the case, a huge role to play— that he didn't notice the car rolling off behind him. A rookie mistake, something he would never do on a normal day.

At the motel, all day long Caramel couldn't get Salt out of her head... and her conscious. She hated that he was dragged into this because of her and wanted no part of the deal anymore. She sat alone in her motel room on a call.

"I don't think I can do this," she said, not for the first time that evening. She twirled her silky hair nervously around her finger, thinking about Salt and the worried look he'd had on his face. She guessed he was right now starting to work it out at the station and didn't trust her anymore.

'Have you forgotten why you agreed to this in the first place?' the voice on the other end asked with a smugness she could almost picture. It was masculine and deep, the kind of voice that gave the impression of one in a brightly colored suit, probably holding a cane and smoking a cigar.

Caramel bit her lip. She knew why, all right. *The money.* It was reason enough for anyone to do anything crazy, and she wouldn't have thought twice about it if it wasn't for... 'The cop, isn't it? That's why you're acting foolish,' the man cut in as if he read her thoughts. 'You're letting your guard down. The one chance you have to leave a life of suffering behind, and you choose to be sentimental?'

"I know what I'm doing, and he doesn't suspect anything." She snapped.

A scornful laughter broke out on the other end. Caramel blushed and lowered her eyes as if the man was right there laughing in front of her. Even she couldn't even believe the words she'd just spoken.

The man's voice became firm. "Get rid of the cop. This is your last chance. You're already in too deep. Think of everything I've ever done for you and everything you've done for me. You'll be rich, okay? And you will be mine. I hate repeating myself." The words were clear: there is no getting out of this.

For a moment, she considered confessing all she knew to Salt, telling him all about the drug operation run through the club, the ruthless takedowns of competitors and the money laundering and how she'd become involved in it because she started to hate the pole and would do anything to leave that life. Once again, the man on the other end seemed to read her thoughts. His voice was harsh and venomous. "Don't even think of crossing me."

The call ended, and Caramel felt overwhelmed by a strong sense of guilt and fear. She had a small gun under the bed, and she had a lot of hate for the world. It wouldn't have been difficult to 'get rid of the cop' if it had been the old her, but now it was a whole lot complicated. There was no happy ending in sight, not at this time. She curled up on the bed and closed her eyes, a familiar wave of loneliness draping over her like a heavy blanket.

The knock rattled her. She'd been dreaming, and it'd been a bad one, so the sudden rap on the door stretched the bad dream into her reality. *They've come!*

The knock came again—a soft tap and then a rap—and she relaxed. She knew who it was. She stood up and went over to the door.

Standing on the tip of her toes, she peered into the hole and saw the detective standing outside. She let out a sigh of relief and caught herself smiling at the sight of him.

After a second of putting on her best poker face, she turned the doorknob hastily and she opened the door.

"Hey," he greeted with a smile. "I'm back."

"Took you forever," she said, rolling her eyes and folding her arms. He entered the room and shut the door behind him. "Are you upset?" he asked. She had her back to him, still pouting.

"I guess I should be happy holed up in this room all day. What am I supposed to do, watch TV?"

"That's not a bad idea," Salt muttered.

"Ugh! So annoying! When can I go back to work?!"

Caramel groaned and rushed to grab a pillow. She tossed it at him, and he easily blocked it. She grabbed another and punted it at him, again without any effect. He chuckled and moved closer while she searched for something else to toss. She almost reached for the bedside lamp when he grabbed her hand and pulled her close.

"Hey, I'm here now, and you're not going anywhere, not at least until I know you're safe," he said softly, wrapping his arms around her. Her lips twitched as she restrained from smiling, or at least tried to.

Her breathing slowed as he pulled her even closer.

"You've been gone all day," she said softly, looking up at him, shuddering slightly, goose bumps prickling through her skin. She wasn't sure if she was cringed out by her own words or if she truly missed the heck out of this handsome man. It was all confusing, but when he came up against her with his tall, strong body and kissed her forehead, it all felt right.

He led her to the bed, and they snuggled and watched cartoons, much to Caramel's surprise. She thought they'd just have sex or something. Instead, he ordered dinner, and they ate and watched silly cartoons. *Where has he been all my life?* She wondered.

"See, TV's not so bad," he said with a teasing laugh. She playfully pinched his arm and settled her head on his chest. "I've never seen a grown man who enjoys cartoons."

"Well, you just met one."

She closed her eyes and savored the moment, and then the sadness was back. She sighed deeply. It wouldn't be long before this was all over.

"What's going on, Delilah? Tell me what's bothering you so much."

She looked up. "You gotta keep that cop habit away from the bedroom."

"Sorry, can't help it. Besides, I know something's up with you. So, tell me, I'm a good listener."

"That's what guys say when they wanna get into your panties," she mused.

"And yet, here I am holding you close, fully clothed." He said proudly. This made her giggle, once again getting a glimpse of why she really liked this guy.

"Nothing," she responded after a short silence. "It all just feels like a dream, like it's too good to be true and that I don't deserve this. I hate that feeling."

"I know they always say when it's too good to be true, it probably is," Salt said, letting his fingers trail alongside her face, stroking it the way she liked. "But let's just assume that it's wrong this time. We can't live life questioning everything that's stressful."

He brought his face closer to hers and brushed his lips over her lips. She smiled and blushed. Soft music played from the TV, the cartoon credits rolling, and it added to the moment.

"You know what I think?" She shook her head.

"Just live every moment as it comes; have fun, enjoy life and be happy. I know it's crazy, but I'm happy whenever we're together. I don't want to overthink it, but I'm really into you."

Eyes glowing, Delilah asked, "What are you saying?" "I care about you…that's what." Salt stated. She smiled as she dug her head into his chest, closing her eyes and lifting the weight of the looming situation off her. She sighed softly as she welcomed some safe slumber in his arms.

Delilah opened her eyes, catching a smile from Salt. It wasn't one of his softer, sexier smiles. It was almost formal. And his eyes were glaring firm and hard at her. He had on his 'cop face'

This rattled her as she sat up.

"What's wrong?" she asked. He sat on a stool next to the bed. On the bedside drawer sat an ashtray filled with several butts of cigarettes, all Delilah's doing (something Salt had made clear that he hated; the excessive smoking), a half-empty bottle of water, brown paper bag of sandwiches —Salt's idea,

Delilah had loved - and the dangling white cord of her iPhone charger. Except, the phone wasn't there. Salt raised his hand, and she caught the glimmer of her purple iPhone in his hand. *What the hell?* She thought with horror, jolting upright, her breasts jiggling from the swift motion.

"What are you doing?" he asked stiffly.

"What…what do you mean?" she responded, her hesitation proving deadly. She narrowed her eyes. "And why are you going through my phone?!" she yelled angrily.

"I'm a detective; it's what I do. I have to be certain you aren't a part of this mess, but it seems to me I may be wrong." In that annoying cop-like fashion, he said the words impersonally, but then he pulled a concerned look on his face and moved closer.

"I'm not going to hurt you, Delilah. I just need to know what you know," he said softly, his voice shifting back to the kind softness she'd found herself missing. "You just have to trust me."

She bit her lip and lowered her head. "I don't know if I can trust you since you apparently like going through people's phones."

"Who's the private number that contacted you over the past few days? It seems it is a consistent occurrence on your phone."

"Do I need a lawyer? You're starting to scare me. And I don't know who that is."

He sighed deeply and held out his hand to her.

She raised her eyebrow as if to ask 'huh?'

After a moment's hesitation, she slid her soft hand into his. This was proving harder than she thought. Why the hell did she think it'd be a good idea to get close with the Detective. She thought it would deter him from the case Now, everything was a mess.

He waited patiently, holding her hand. Giving her a gentle nod with his head to implore her to trust him. She sighed softly and closing her eyes, she spoke the words out loud. "Okay, I'll tell you what I know."

Salt smiled.

Delilah's eyes watered, and it annoyed her. *Don't go all soft now*, she told herself. But it was hard; no one had ever spoken to her the way Salt did and the comfort he gave. She'd had people tell her they loved her, but she knew those men were faking it, and all they wanted was to use her for their own personal pleasure. Not Salt; she could tell he meant it just by looking at him. And *damn it*, she thought, *I care about him too.* "I have to tell you something. It's about the case." She confessed

He leaned in close, catching that look of terror on her face. "But I...well, it's not safe and—"

Salt glanced up when he heard a sound. He sat upright and was about to reach for his gun when the door swung open, and a couple of guys stormed into the room.

He jumped to his feet, throwing the covers off and instinctively blocking Delilah. The men were dressed in street clothes and heavily armed with blood-red eyes.

They meant business, alright. "Oh, come on. déjà vu, really?" Salt said with a groan as if the presence of the armed men was too much of an inconvenience.

"Good thing I'm not naked." He quipped

"Making jokes, huh?" one of the men muttered, stepping forward. He swung his fist at Salt, who ducked swiftly and hammered a blow into the man's rock-solid gut. The man grunted and rolled over, eyes twitching as Salt punched his face and knocked him out.

The body stiffened on the ground, but the others didn't seem bothered. They had guns, and it was duly pointed at the cop. "Once again, I have to clean up your mess, Caramel," a familiar voice said. Salt looked. It was Zack, Caramel's boss. Zack shook his head as he approached Salt. "You're a pain in the butt, you know that right?" he looked up at Caramel, saw her near nakedness and shook his head. "And as for you- you're stupid. Just a whore at heart. Thought I could trust you."

Salt turned to Delilah, shocked.

Zack roared with a hoarse laughter. "What, you thought the bitch cared about you? Oh, please. She's been working for me, and you fell right into our trap."

He walked over to her and squeezed her jaw. "Too bad she became weak. What the hell, how'd you let this cop sway you?" Zack scoffed and switched his gaze between the hurt Salt and the stunned Caramel. "I guess he is handsome. But whatever. I have a mind to kill him now and—" "Don't hurt him!" Caramel screamed.

One of the men stood over Salt and smashed his head with the butt of his gun, just for the heck of it. Salt crashed to the ground, everything blurring around him, the sounds slowly fading away. In that last moment, just before it became dark, he thought to himself how much of a fool he'd been.

Chapter 6

S alt was tied up to a chair in a warehouse when he came back to consciousness, his head felt like a street hammered by a marching band, and the side of his face was sore and swollen. The guy in the corner holding a bloodied bat, a grin on his face, certainly looked like the culprit. Salt tasted blood inside his mouth, and the aching in his ribs bothered him. The door opened slowly, and Zack appeared first, followed surprisingly by the man named Antonio Bruselli. *The mogul and do-good businessman? I've seen him so many times at hospital openings and charity auctions! Is this who we've been looking for all this time?* Thundered Salt in his mind— *it is* him, the drug lord they'd been after for many years—and Caramel. Bruselli had his arm around her waist. She wore a tight, black, skimpy silk dress and a scared frown.

Their eyes met, and she knew what he was thinking. She wanted to scream and let him know this wasn't the plan; she wanted him to believe her.

Bruselli stepped forward. He was a suited-up man with slicked back dark wavy hair and a charismatic smirk, ruthless and smug. He was also wealthy and dangerous, with most of the city in his pocket. And here he was, grinning like the devil. Salt held his gaze with guts.

"Let me tell you a little story," Bruselli said, smiling.

"I wasn't always the 'bad guy', but that's how the story goes." He explained that he started off with good intentions. A man with an eye for business and a natural power over people, it had only taken him a couple of years to be a successful businessman. Real estate to fabrics, high demand produces to grain exports. He did everything. He felt the obligation to give back. Being from a poor family of immigrants, he knew what it meant to be handicapped by society. He gave to multiple charities, built hospitals and all that. But the money was never enough.

He had bought a large plantation in Brazil, hidden deep in the rainforest, blanketed by thick shrubs and dense jungle. He had taken it off the hands of a local merchant. To everyone else, it would be a bad investment- too far away for home- but Bruselli saw potential in it to set up a large coffee plantation for cheap. He had a positive business plan, not until the cartel approached him. That was many years ago. They appealed to the money side of him, and he couldn't say no to such a prospect. A runway was built right on his land, and acres were converted to drug crops. A cargo plane flew in once a week to pack the shipment of drugs. Because of who he was and who he knew, it wasn't hard to bribe the officials and make them look the other way, and soon Bruselli became drunk with power and even more wealthy. The money flowed in faster than it could be counted.

With Massoni stationed in the States, his job was to pump the drugs through the strip club and, with any excess distributed on the streets, to market the strip club as the source to get more.

Easy. Like honey to the bees.

"It was a perfect operation until you..." he paused and clenched his fists. "You have been the little prick who's been a pain in my ass," Brusselli said.

"I got you now, don't I? Thanks to Caramel here. She played you like an *idiota,* and you fell for it," he said with his heavy Italian accent.

Quickly, Bruselli turned to Caramel, a grave look in his eyes. "Here's the thing, my friend," Bruselli went on, "you can have all the money in the world and still be powerless under the whims of a beauty like her." He squeezed her cheeks and looked into her eyes. "In this business, you always have to watch your back, or else someone will trample on you and use you as a stepping stone. Caramel, well, she's my most prized asset. I set her on my competition; they're vulnerable even before they know it. That is how I keep everyone in check. And you, an annoying pest that you are, also fell for it. I gotta say, she is pretty good. Seductive and sexy, like Cleopatra, you know: capable of falling an empire with her beauty or hey even like Delilah from the Bible... ha! Isn't that something?" he roared with laughter

"It can be poetic, don't you think? I mean, I shouldn't be here but the series of bad news I keep getting, well, it makes me unhappy."

Bruselli's intense gaze was fixed on Caramel. "As for you- I asked you to take care of him. There is a reason I send you those texts, and that reason is so that I don't have to be here!" he snapped, his voice like a roar.

So, he was the one sending the texts? Caramel changed his contact name to Zack's to protect him Salt thought at that moment.

He's so confident I'm going to die; he's blabbing out everything.

"What are you looking at?" Bruselli growled at Salt. One of his men landed a punch on Salt's face.

Caramel whimpered, and this caught Bruselli's attention. "You went soft on him, though. I don't like that. You were MY girl. Now you're his whore!!"

He suddenly growled and smacked her in the face. Salt flinched and rushed forward, but the bonds around his body restrained him, and the chair merely creaked. Zack took a shock step back, and Bruselli merely smiled.

"Throw them in the cell. Have each other. They deserve each other. By morning, we will take care of them. I must give a speech soon at a fundraiser. Cannot have blood on my hands while I try to collect some money from the masses." he ordered, again like some kind of villain from an old-school movie. Except, this was real, and they could die.

Caramel looked at Salt, sobbing at the sight of the bruises on his face. He breathed heavily, his head down. She tried to talk to him, but he ignored her.

"I'm so sorry," she whispered to him, sobbing quietly. "I just couldn't tell you. Damnit! I didn't expect things to get so complicated. I care for you, too; I swear I do. I just wish everything was different."

Salt raised his head. "Don't cuss," he said, a smile on his face.

"It's not ladylike."

Caramel sniffled and suppressed a laugh. She went over to him and embraced him. "Aren't you mad at me?"

"Oh, I am. Pissed off, even. But we can always handle that later. But I need you to tell me something," he said, and she looked at him with concern.

She nodded.

"Do you still have those texts Bruselli sent you?"

She nodded. "Yes. He always texted me whenever he needed something done. I was indebted to him, so I would just do as he ordered. Go to this hotel and seduce this guy, stuff like that. The men almost always end up dead, but...but I didn't mean..." her voice cracked and trailed off.

"Hey," Salt said softly. She looked up. "Now's not the time to cry. Maybe later, okay?" he smiled, and she also smiled, sniffling, and wiping off the tears.

Salt looked around the cell, his mind ticking. "Bruselli's here. I need to find a way to call HQ. I just need a distraction. We have the big dog in our hands; we must find a way to chain him." "Leave that to me," Caramel said, her eyes sparkling, a sly smile on her face. Salt felt a rush, his member hardening just at the sight of that. *Focus,* he told himself.

"Hey, assholes, I think this man's dead!" Caramel suddenly screamed. Salt quickly lay on the ground.

Disgruntled voices outside the cell drew closer. The iron door creaked open, and two men stepped in. They walked over to Salt and poked him, mumbling to themselves.

Salt suddenly leaped up and grabbed the gun, pointing at him. He pulled hard, the man went stumbling, and then he knocked him out with an elbow to the face. "Hey!" the other guy yelled, trying to react. Caramel grabbed the wooden chair on the far side of the room and smashed it on the guy's head.

"Good job!" Salt said. Caramel blushed. He asked her to stay behind while he looked for the other guards in the building. She whispered that she wanted to help, but he assured her she would be safer on the bench. Salt counted all the guards that were there, so he knew, as he managed to call for backup with a phone snagged from the guy knocked out. Several of the guards were outside smoking and drinking, looking bored.

Bruselli wasn't in the building; unsurprisingly, he was quick to show up at the fundraiser for the new museum, but he seemed to have the fun idea of an execution for the next day.

The wonder cop with the weird name, who'd been giving him hell, would finally be taken care of. It took a couple of minutes for Salt to call for backup. If they wanted to nail Bruselli, they'd have to flush him out, which meant coming up with a plan. "We can just leave now, get away from all this," Caramel said desperately, tugging his hand. She had a bad feeling about the plan, and sticking around could mean he'd get killed. He assured her that he wouldn't be alone.

It didn't take long for the place to be surrounded. Salt got up as soon as the lights flashed outside. Chaotic voices rushed through the air, and soon, the rapid sound of gunfire rocked the place. It lasted just a few minutes, and then silence followed. Caramel slipped away during the chaos, certain that she would also get arrested.

Chapter 7

It took a couple of months for Bruselli and his operation to be taken down. Caramel had disappeared. Salt was assigned a new case, and he had to force himself to move on and forget her. It was for the best, he told himself. If only he had gotten to say a proper goodbye, though.

The days seemed slow now, and everything had a drab feeling to it. Work was good, sure, but the thorough enjoyment he felt had evaporated. He was obsessed with thoughts of Caramel, and this baffled him. He buried himself in work, coming home late, all in a bid to forget. And then it all changed with a simple text from an unknown number late one night.

I want to see you again. How about tomorrow night 9pm at the motel in the same room? It's been forever.

He smiled as soon as he read the text, knowing exactly who it was from. Just a few words but he read them over and over. He felt that surge of excitement as he thought about meeting Caramel again.

As he opened the door. She stood there, her eyes shining with unshed tears and a smile that lit up her face. In her white t-shirt and blue tight-fitting jeans, with her long dark brown hair clipped back with a few strands at the front - just like how he first saw her. The real her...Delilah. Without a word, they rushed into each other's arms, embracing as if time never got away from them.

Their kisses were sweet and desperate, fueled by the overwhelming desire to be close once more. No more lies, no more explanations. Their hands roamed each other's bodies, reacquainting themselves with every curve and line.

Finally, they broke apart, their breath coming in short gasps as they gazed into each other's eyes. The longing they saw mirrored back at them only deepened their connection, igniting a fire that could not be contained.

Without a word, Salt took Delilah's hand and led her into their motel room, the anticipation building with each step. Once inside, they fell onto the bed in a tangle of limbs and slow kisses. In the privacy of their room, the atmosphere was ripe with a mix of excitement and tenderness. Delilah pulled herself away and moved off the bed. *Time to show him what I have for him.*

Delilah stood at the end of the bed, her eyes meeting Salt's with a playful spark. Slowly, she reached for the hem of her t-shirt, teasingly lifting it inch by inch. Smiling wickedly, Salt's gaze followed her movements. She was in no hurry, savoring the moment, feeling the electric tension building between them.

With a final, deliberate motion, Delilah pulled the t-shirt over her head, revealing the stunning lingerie beneath. The delicate black lace of the brasserie clung to her curves, accentuating her figure in all the right places. She used her hands to pull down her jeans swiftly and reveal the entire lingerie set against her gorgeous body. The bra's intricate design highlighted her cleavage, while the matching panties sat perfectly on her hips, adding an air of sophistication and seduction.

Salt's eyes widened with admiration and desire. The lingerie was a surprise, something Delilah had chosen carefully, knowing how much he would appreciate the gesture.

As Delilah took a step closer, Salt reached out, his fingers brushing against the lace, marveling at the softness of the fabric and the warmth of her skin beneath. He stood up and pulled her gently towards him, their bodies aligning perfectly.

They shared a passionate kiss, Salt's hands roamed over her back, his touch sending shivers down Delilah's spine. She responded by pressing closer, her fingers threading through his slicked-back hair, pulling him deeper into her.

As the moonlight filtered through the sheer curtains of the motel room, casting a soft blue glow across the room, their eyes met, and a silent understanding passed between them. He pulled back to take a good look at her.

"You are so beautiful," he whispered, his voice husky with emotion. He reached out to her holding the side of her face. He never wanted her memory or this moment to fade.

They stood in silence for a moment, letting the reality of their reunion sink in.

She smiled, a blush rising to her cheeks, and leaned into his touch. Their lips met in another slow, tender kiss.

With gentle care and a deep desire to have her, he started the intimate act by soft slow kisses on the side of her neck. He smiled when she shivered, knowing it made her ticklish, as he went on he could hear her moan soft, and see her eyes go almost sleepy.

His kisses trailed down her neck, each one slow, as if he were committing every inch of her to his memory. Delilah's breath fastened, her body responding to his touch with a mix of anticipation and desire. She could feel the tenderness in his every movement, the way he cherished her.

Salt continued his journey downward, his lips tracing a path over her collarbone, across her shoulders, and down the length of her body. His hands caressed her skin with the lightest of touches, making her shiver with delight. There was no rush, only the slow, unhurried exploration of her, a silent exchange of trust and affection.

When he reached her hips, Salt paused, his eyes meeting hers once more, seeking her comfort in every step. With a loving smile, he gently slipped his fingers beneath the fabric of her underwear, his touch reverent as he slowly removed them. Delilah's heart raced, not just from the anticipation of what was to come, but from the overwhelming sense of being loved so completely.

As he directed her to the edge of the bed, he laid her down as he knelt in front of her, Salt pressed soft kisses to her inner thigh, a silent promise of the pleasure and intimacy they were about to share. Delilah closed her eyes, spread her legs wider letting herself get lost in the moment, in the passion that flowed between them.

Delilah's breath hitched as Salt's lips and tongue continued their slow, deliberate dance over her most sensitive places, her body responding to him with waves of pleasure. Every movement, every touch was infused with the tenderness that had always defined their connection. She reached down, her fingers threading through his hair, silently urging him on, her body trembling under his care.

Salt took his time, savoring the taste and feel of her, listening to every sound she made, every gasp and moan that told him he was bringing her closer to the edge.

But just as the tension in her body began to peak, he slowly eased back, his lips leaving her skin as he kissed his way back up her body.

Their eyes met, and the connection between them was electric, filled with a mutual understanding of what they both wanted and needed. Salt paused to kiss her deeply, their mouths moving together in perfect harmony as their bodies aligned. After he released himself from his zipper, He guided himself to her entrance, and for a moment, they hovered on the edge, savoring the anticipation.

With a slow, steady motion, Salt entered her, his movements careful, deliberate, as he looked to prolong the sensation, to make every moment last. Delilah's hands clutched his shoulders, her body arching to meet his, every inch of her welcoming him inside.

They moved together as if they had never been apart, as if their bodies had memorized the rhythm of their love. Each thrust, each gasp was a testament to the depth of their connection, the passion that had not dimmed despite the time and distance. It was more than just physical; it was the reaffirmation of their bond, a silent promise that no matter how far apart they were, they would always come back together.

As they reached the peak of their passion, they held onto each other tightly, not wanting to let go, not wanting to lose the feeling of completeness they had found again. Their release was a shared moment of ecstasy, a culmination of all the emotions they had kept bottled up inside but a celebration of the strong bond they shared from everything that they have been through together.

Breathless and spent, "Hold me," she whispered in a strained voice and held out her arms to him. He held her so close, and they embraced.

As they lay entwined beneath the soft sheets, their breathing gradually slowed, syncing with the gentle rhythm of their hearts. The warmth of their bodies lingered in the space between them, a gentle reminder of the closeness they'd just shared. He pulled her closer, his hand tracing lazy patterns on her back, and she nestled into the crook of his arm, feeling safe and cherished. The world outside faded as their eyelids grew heavy, and with a final whispered "I love you," they drifted into the peaceful embrace of sleep, still wrapped in the afterglow of their love.

Salt expected her to be gone when he woke up, it was all too good to be true, but she was right there in his arms. He kissed her lips, and she smiled and opened her eyes.

"I thought you'd leave," he said.

"I don't want to leave. There's no point in leaving."

She sat up and frowned deeply. He also sat up, leaning against the bed frame.

"You'll have to testify against Massoni and Bruselli. And that will make you a target."

She smiled a wry smile and reached for a cigarette, the bedsheet sliding off and exposing her beautiful bosom. He helped her light up, and she smiled faintly. After a few puffs, her eyes became hard-set, and her lips tightened.

"I know. And I'm ready to testify."

The look of fear came back as she turned and looked at Salt. "But what if I get sentenced too? I never sold any drugs. I know I got my hands dirty, but I was just...used. I had no choice."

He reached out and gave her hand a reassuring squeeze. "You will be under protective custody throughout the trial, and I'll make sure you get a good deal out of this. You will be able to start a new life, and the bad guys will just be shadows in the past."

She smiled and kissed him. "It would all be so perfect if that new life had you in it."

THE END

About the Author

Natasha Rose is a new author with a penchant for erotica and romance. As a full-time Mum, she dreams the day away about adventures and endless passion. Until one day, she decided to put ideas to paper and make her dreams come true.

This was bound to happen as creative writing is in Natasha's true nature. At the tender age of 15, she was awarded a distinction in a writing contest by NSW University.

Although thankful for her escapism, she is incredibly grateful for her role as a homemaker, cooking and gardening for her husband and their son.